# The Birds
## of
# Bethlehem

## Tomie dePaola

NANCY PAULSEN BOOKS ❧ AN IMPRINT OF PENGUIN GROUP (USA) INC.

Every morning,
the birds of Bethlehem
gathered in the field to
glean any corn that might
be left from the harvest.

This winter morning was different.
Anyone watching would have thought
that they spent more time talking to
one another than having breakfast.

And that was true.

"Yesterday afternoon, we saw something we'd never seen before," said the green bird and his mate.

"We saw a long line of people coming over the hills."

The yellow bird and his mate spoke up.
"We saw something very unusual
yesterday as well."

"The inn in town was full."

"What we saw," said the blue bird and his mate, "was very strange indeed."

"A man and his wife were led to the stable because there was no room left at the inn."

"We were roosting in a tree on the hill," said the red bird and his mate. "Below us, there were shepherds watching their sheep. We saw an extraordinary thing."

"An Angel appeared in the sky and said,
'I bring you tidings of great joy.
Go quickly to Bethlehem, where you
will find a baby lying in a manger.'"

"We were in the same tree," said the brown bird
and his mate. "And what we saw was spectacular."

"The night sky was filled with heavenly hosts singing:

'Glory to God in the highest
And on earth peace to men of goodwill.' "

"What we saw," said the white bird and his mate, "was an awesome sight, so we followed the shepherds."

"Let us go see this miraculous thing that
has come to pass," all the birds agreed.

In the stable was a young mother,
her husband and their newborn baby.

For Sister Veronique
and the Community of Redwoods Monastery

NANCY PAULSEN BOOKS • A division of Penguin Young Readers Group.

Published by The Penguin Group.

Penguin Group (USA) Inc., 375 Hudson Street, New York, NY 10014, U.S.A.

Penguin Group (Canada), 90 Eglinton Avenue East, Suite 700, Toronto, Ontario M4P 2Y3, Canada

(a division of Pearson Penguin Canada Inc.).

Penguin Books Ltd, 80 Strand, London WC2R 0RL, England.

Penguin Ireland, 25 St. Stephen's Green, Dublin 2, Ireland (a division of Penguin Books Ltd).

Penguin Group (Australia), 250 Camberwell Road, Camberwell, Victoria 3124, Australia

(a division of Pearson Australia Group Pty Ltd).

Penguin Books India Pvt Ltd, 11 Community Centre, Panchsheel Park, New Delhi - 110 017, India.

Penguin Group (NZ), 67 Apollo Drive, Rosedale, Auckland 0632, New Zealand (a division of Pearson New Zealand Ltd).

Penguin Books (South Africa) (Pty) Ltd, 24 Sturdee Avenue, Rosebank, Johannesburg 2196, South Africa.

Penguin Books Ltd, Registered Offices: 80 Strand, London WC2R 0RL, England.

Design by Marikka Tamura.

Text set in Estilo Script and Arta Std.

The art was done in opaque acrylics on Arches 180 lb. handmade watercolor paper.

Library of Congress Cataloging-in-Publication Data is available upon request.

DePaola, Tomie, 1934–

The birds of Bethlehem / Tomie dePaola. p. cm.

Summary: On the morning of the first Christmas, the colorful birds of Bethlehem gather to talk about the exciting events they

have witnessed, from the long line of people approaching the town to the stable where a newborn baby lies.

1. Jesus Christ—Nativity—Juvenile fiction. [1. Jesus Christ—Nativity—Fiction. 2. Birds—Fiction.] I. Title.

PZ7.D439Bk 2012   [E]—dc23   2011046802

ISBN 978-0-399-25780-3

1 3 5 7 9 10 8 6 4 2